KRISTEN DOVNIK
Ruthless Pride
A Lion King Retelling

Ruthless Pride

For all the girlies who were in love with the

Badass Lion

Chapter 1

Kiara age 16

The humid atmosphere is heavy with anticipation as sweaty bodies slide up against me. Ewww, they're so disgusting! Hundreds of people have gathered here tonight, waiting eagerly to see who will be crowned the champion. All eyes are fixed on the ring in the centre of the arena, where two men are about to face off. Grandfather's prized fighter rushes forward and punches his opponent in the side of the face, making his head snap to the left. Blood sprays from his mouth, landing on the floor not too far from where I'm sitting.

"Yes! Get him, Nuka!" my father shouts. My body tingles all over as I stare up at the ring. After waiting eight long months, it's hard to believe that we are finally here. Our confidence in Nuka is unwavering, as he has remained the undefeated champion throughout the entire season. My grandfather Mufasa has promised him a substantial sum of money and a well-deserved vacation if he pulls through and secures a victory for us in this final fight.

My great uncle Scar stands beside his brother cheering on our mighty warrior. In fact, our entire entourage is here tonight to witness this. Nuka lands a few more blows against Rook's abdomen while the boxer protects his face. He's backed into a corner with nowhere to go and Nuka continues throwing punches, never allowing his opponent even a second to breathe.

"Knock him out!" I yell and then instantly feel my father's eyes of approval on the side of my face. I glance over and see him smiling from ear to ear. He is proud that I finally decided to come watch a match. I wasn't keen on seeing the others, they were smaller and not as grand as this one. Also, I was a little afraid that Nuka wouldn't make it and then I'd have to listen to Grandfather whinge and bitch the whole way home. It was a hard pass from me and luckily for him, he never lost.

Rook lowers his right arm out of sight before quickly raising it and uppercuts Nuka in the jaw. The whole arena boos with distaste as they watch their victor fall back against the mat. The ref moves to Nuka's side as Rook climbs on top of him.

The ref smashes his fist against the mat, "One... Two... Three... Pinned!" he yells. Shit, that's not good. I glance over at my grandfather on my left and watch him pinch his lips together as he stares angrily at his fighter. Oh, I would hate to be Nuka right about now.

"Hey baby girl, take this and go get yourself a drink." My father leans over my mother, handing me a twenty before glancing back at his dad. I think we can all see the shit show that's about to go down and I definitely don't want to be around to see that.

I pocket the twenty and begin to move my way through the crowd, Bruce, my bodyguard, following closely behind me. There are so many people shouting and screaming near the side of the ring that it's almost impossible for me to make my way through. Bruce never steps in to lend a hand as he likes me to learn how to fend for myself. What great help he is... not!

A tall boy with broad shoulders comes to my rescue as he shoves an older man with a huge belly out of the way. The man grumbles as he stumbles backwards but says nothing once he sees who I am and which direction I just came from. Although my parents are concerned about what my grandfather will do to his fighter, I have no doubt that they are still watching me. Their predatory nature never seems to elude them. Another man stumbles into me and again the tall boy pushes him away. I don't even have to look up to know it's Kovu, Scar's favourite assassin's son. He has a tendency to follow me wherever I go whether I like it or not.

He clears the path ahead of me before stepping to the side. "The path's clear, Your Highness," he jokes with a smile on his face. His brown eyes twinkle with mischief but I can see right through him.

"Oh piss off, why don't you." I barge past him, taking the steps two at a time until I reach the top. My heart hammers in my chest as I try walking off my sudden exhaustion. Who knew the arena had so many damn steps. I glance over my shoulder to where my parents are by the side of the ring. They look like tiny ants from all the way up here.

"If you wanted to play a game of chase, you could have just asked," Kovu says in a low voice behind me. He is so close that his heat seeps into my back.

"When will you get it through your thick skull that I am trying to get away from you," I huff as I turn and continue walking towards the canteen. The line for refreshments is insane. It's going to take me ages to get through. I move to the back of the line and grab my phone out of my pocket. I feel multiple sets of eyes staring at me, but I try to not let them see that I care. I know some of them probably know who I am, and how could they not? My face is regularly plastered all over the news. "The heir to the Pride family fortune once again out past her bedtime," the headlines say. Stupid tabloids! For once I just wish they would leave me alone. It sucks being in line to take over the family business. It's mine whether I want it or not.

The Prides are well known for their illegal activities, the guns, the girls and especially the drugs. We are the biggest drug cartel in the southern hemisphere and yet the cops can't touch us. I swear my grandparents pay the corrupt ones off or something bad happens and then once again we make headlines.

"So instead of talking to me you would rather watch dogs jumping through hoops?" Kovu asks over my shoulder.

"Damn straight I would. They are a hell of a lot more interesting than you," I mutter, never taking my eyes off my screen.

"Whatever," Kovu huffs as he looks away. Thankfully I won't have to be near him much longer, this line seems to be moving relatively quickly. Two girls further up keep turning around and giggling as they stare at the black-headed boy over my shoulder. What is it about him that makes all the girls go crazy?

Is it his dreamy eyes or is it the way he always seems to be smiling even when he's not? I shake my head. My father warned me countless times to watch myself around him. His mother Zira is a notorious assassin, who's to say she hasn't taught him to be exactly like her?

A minute or two passes before it's my turn to step up to the counter. "A large lemon soda please and can I get it with no ice. Thanks."

"And I'll have the same, please," Kovu mutters behind me and I feel my blood begin to boil. I think I've had just about as much as I can take from him today. Why does he have to also hover around me like a little bug? Why can't he just piss off and play with his own friends? Maybe he doesn't have any. That wouldn't surprise me—if he acts this way around me, god knows how he would around them.

The cashier quickly rushes off without taking our money and I frown. "I'm not paying for yours," I declare as I turn back to look at him. He smiles from ear to ear and I wish I could just punch him in the face.

"I didn't expect you to." He leans forward and scans his card against the card reader, ultimately paying for both of us.

"Why did you do that? I could easily pay for myself, you know." I hold up the twenty and wave it in front of his face. He swats my hand away and stares up at the scoreboard above our heads. Nuka won round one with a three point lead however lost round two by two points. He needs to get his ass back up in the game and win round three or it's over for all of us. Grandfather will send him to the south, and no one ever returns from the outlands. Once you disgrace the Prides' family name, that's it, you're gone, there are no second chances.

"Yeah, you could have, but I beat you to it." The cashier rushes over with our drinks and thrusts them towards us. I eagerly grab mine and move aside for the next person in line.

"You're an asshole," I mutter before taking a sip of my drink. With Kovu by my side and my bodyguard not too far away, we weave our way through the throngs of people as we make our way over to the staircase leading back down into the arena.

"Who just bought you a drink? Maybe you should give me a kiss on the cheek as payment instead of being mean to me." Kovu moves his face closer to mine and for a second I really think I'm going to punch him. Why would I pay him when I didn't want him to buy the drink in the first place?

"Or maybe, I should just kick your ass." I turn my face and glare up at him. If Nuka loses tonight, maybe Grandfather will allow me and Kovu a chance to enter the ring. I sure would love to show him what

I have been practising for all these years. The muscles in my arms twitch with excitement.

"Now, now, princess, no need to get feisty. We are all friends here…" BANG! Instinctively I drop to the floor, spilling my drink all over the step beside me. What the fuck was that?! Screams of terror charge towards me as people begin running up the steps towards us. Crap! I'm about to be trampled. I move slightly to the side, trying to avoid those wanting to escape. My heart hammers in my chest as I look up at the screens above the ring to see Nuka with a gun in his hand, pointed directly at my grandfather.

"NO!" I scream as he pulls the trigger and the bullet hits Mufasa square in the chest. Blood spews from the gaping wound and slides down the front of his immaculate brown suit.

Mufasa's lifeless body falls to the floor as Nuka swings his loaded gun towards my parents. Zira stands behind my father with a knife in hand. She raises it to his throat as another gunshot ricochets throughout the room. I move my hands to cover my ears but I can't tear my eyes away from the murder that is happening right now. Zira pulls the knife swiftly to the right, slicing my father's jugular, spilling his blood for all to see. The camera slightly shows my mother on his right with a bullet wound between her eyes. NO!! My whole body screams as my body goes weak.

Tears stream down my face as my family's dead bodies are broadcast live on every screen around the arena. Why have they not been turned off already!? Someone is tugging my arm but I can't move, I can't breathe. They are gone... All three of them... Gone. BANG! Pain as I've never felt before shoots across my chest as my body is thrown back against the staircase. Ouch. It takes me a good moment to realise I've been shot.

"FUCK!" Kovu yells, lifting my limp body from the ground, and begins carrying me up the stairs. I cry out from the sudden movement, but he doesn't hear me. "It wasn't meant to be this way. They promised me you wouldn't get hurt." He knew this would happen and said nothing? Warmth spreads across the front of my shirt as the tips of my fingers and toes start to feel cold. Kovu reaches the landing we were on moments ago and breaks into a run. I would place my hand over my heart, but I can barely move. Am I going to die?

"GET OUT OF THE WAY!!" Kovu yells and those in front of us move, allowing him to run straight out the front door.

"Your mother killed my dad," I whisper, looking up at him. He doesn't even look at me as he turns right and sprints us towards the under-rail bridge. The homeless and drug addicts dwell beneath the heavy metal that carries the trains high above. My father walked me through the slums years ago—he wanted me to learn all about the family business and what it does to the people who live down here. My father never agreed with the way we made our money. He said we should never profit off someone else's pain. Addiction is a horrible thing to endure, but without it, the Prides' family fortune would cease to be.

My father had plans to change so many things once he took over, but thanks to Zira, he will never get the chance.

I start to shiver as my body turns cold and yet Kovu doesn't stop here. He continues to run until we reach the other end of the slums. He places me carefully on the ground before removing his jacket and covering my body with it.

"It's going to be alright, Kiara. You're safe now," Kovu mutters, saying it more to himself than to me.

"Your mother killed my father." I repeat the same words as before and this time he hears me. His eyes turn down as he stares at my blood-soaked shirt peeking out from beneath his jacket.

"I know, Kiara, and I'm so sorry. It wasn't supposed to go down like that." He retrieves his phone from his pocket and quickly enters a number. Someone answers on the first ring and immediately begins yelling at him through the phone. "I know, alright, but forget about that for now, Kiara needs help. She was shot in the chest and I can't stay here to help her. Zira probably already knows I got her out and she'll be looking for us. I hid her the best I could underneath the rail bridge, south side of the arena. To find her, enter through the main gates, head right to the end and then take a left. You need to hurry though. I don't know how much longer she will be able to hold on." Kovu hangs up without saying goodbye and drops to his knees in front of me. "Help is on the way," he says, lifting the front of my shirt just enough to see the wound. I grit my teeth as pain shoots through my chest, but he doesn't stop. He tears a length of material away from the bottom of his shirt, rolls it into a ball and shoves it into the hole. I scream out in agony as he fiddles with the placement but thankfully, once he is satisfied the bleeding has slowed, he places my shirt back where it was before.

"I'm going to kill you," I whisper as I am not able to speak any louder. Tears well in the corners of my eyes from all the rage and adrenaline coursing through me. I hate them. I hate all of them. His mother took my father away from me and if I was strong enough right now, I would take her prized son away from her. I would rip him to shreds and make her regret the day she ever met me.

"You just get better first okay, but I have to go. The boys will be here soon, they will help you. I'm so sorry I can't do more, this was never meant to happen, they promised me you wouldn't get hurt." Fuck him for being so sweet, but I see right through his facade. Kovu has always been the type of guy to cover his own ass, he's thrown me under the bus a few times before. He opens his mouth to say more just as his phone starts ringing. His pupils dilate as he glances down at the screen. "Fuck," he whispers. His gaze shoots back the way we came, thankfully no one is there. "I have to go, Kiara. It's not safe for you if I stay any longer. Mother is on the hunt, I have to lure her away. Please get better, I'll come find you when the time is right. I'm so sorry." He leans forward and places a gentle kiss on my forehead before getting to his feet and sprints off. What the fuck was that?! Why did he kiss me?

My head feels like bricks on my shoulders, it's so heavy. I raise my chin and rest the back of my skull against the wall behind me. Ah, that's better. A tear slides down the side of my cheek as the memory of my father's blood-soaked shirt plays over and over in my mind. My chest aches, not only from the pain of my wound but the emptiness in my heart. My whole family is gone, taken away from me forever. Who will come for me now? I have no one left. Kovu said the boys would come, but that could be anyone. I close my eyes and wish for the end. I want it all to go away. The vision of my mother's golden hair blowing in the afternoon breeze as she smiles at me is the only thing I want to see until the pearly white gates above me open up and swallow me whole. I'm ready for this life to end.

Chapter 2

It feels like hours have passed when the sound of heavy footsteps approaching quickly filters through my ears. It bloody took them long enough. I swear if these were my henchmen and I sent them to take care of a job for me, I would expect them to do it much quicker than this. Unless it's Zira coming herself. She is the type of woman who likes to make sure the job is complete. The footsteps get closer and instinctively I hold my breath. They slow down a short distance away but I can still hear them moving around frantically.

"Oh shit!" A familiar voice calls out. I try to raise my head away from the wall, but I can't. The muscles in my neck have practically disappeared—or maybe I've lost so much blood that my body is now dying. "Hurry up Pumba, she's over here!" Timon rushes to my side and a sense of relief floods through me. They came for me. My father's oldest friends came to save me. Is this who Kovu rang? Why did he ring them and not my father's guards?

Timon tentatively checks for signs of life by placing his fingers under my jaw. He holds them there for a few seconds and then lets out a sigh of relief. "You're still with us, baby girl," he whispers under his breath. Another set of footsteps, heavier than the ones before, approaches and stops directly beside me. "She's alive, but barely. We have to get her to the compound quickly, Raf will fix her up."

"Wouldn't a hospital be a better option? You know, as the compound is much further away." Pumba slides his arms under my legs and around my back, lifting me off the ground. An agonising grunt vibrates in my throat as the pain in my chest intensifies by the sudden movement. Pumba stumbles a few steps, however he corrects himself quickly and we begin to travel back through the slums at a rapid pace. My head hangs back as my left arm flops around all over the place. My body begins to shiver and there is nothing I can do to stop it.

"A hospital would also be the first place a killer would look if they believed their victim was still alive. I swear sometimes you faked your way through Rafiki's training." My father told me about those days when he used to train day and night with Raf. He had a lot of disputes with his father while growing up and Raf helped him learn how to channel his anger. Long before I was born, Dad used to spend so much time down at the compound that Mum practically had to drag him back to the Pride estate. I don't think he went back down there much after that.

"Oh yeah, I didn't think about that, but you're also still jealous that I received better scores than you." Pumba puffs out his chest as much as he can. Timon scoffs beside us as we dash through the exit out of the slums.

"I am not. You only won half the time because you are double my weight in muscle. I had no hope of sparring against you." My eyelids begin to feel heavy the closer we get to Pumba's van, which is parked on the other side of the street. There are so many people running around, I am amazed no one tried to stop us and we were able to move through freely. "Hey baby girl, stay with us, okay? It won't take us long to get to the compound, but you have to stay awake, okay? Can you do that?" Concern lingers in Timon's voice as he opens the side door and Pumba places me carefully on the floor.

"I'm so cold," I breathe and my shivering intensifies the second Pumba lets me go. He was so warm, but I don't think I'm shivering from the cold anymore. I've lost so much blood I think my body is going into shock. One of them grabs me a blanket as the other jumps in the driver's seat. The second the door is shut we race off up the street. For a second my eyes flutter open to see Timon staring down at me. He has his hands pressed against my chest trying to stop the blood from pouring out. Pumba has his foot flat on the gas and presses the horn whenever someone gets in our way. "Fucking move why don't you!" he growls to those slowing us down.

Timon removes a hand from my chest and pulls something out of his pocket. The click of a phone being unlocked sounds next to my ear, followed by a ringer. "Hey Raf, we found her but she is in really bad shape. The bullet got her in the chest. If I'm being honest, we were lucky to have found her alive." He pauses and there is a muffled response coming from the other end. "Yeah, I'm pretty sure her file would be there. Simba would have made sure you had a copy just in case." Pumba takes a sharp turn, causing me to wince from the pain shooting through my body. I feel myself slide in and out of consciousness. Timon keeps repeating we are almost there but I don't know how much longer I can hold on. "Hurry the fuck up Pumba, we're losing her!" he growls.

"Fuck off! I'm going as fast as I can!" Pumba yells back. He takes another sharp turn but this time I am too far gone to make a noise as agony slices through me. *'It's okay to let go, baby girl, I'm right here,'* my dad's voice whispers above me. I see his smiling face looking down as he reaches his hand out towards me. I grasp it and allow him to lift me up. I am weightless like a feather as I float through the air right above where I lay on the floor.

'But they will be sad if I die,' I retort, looking down at Timon from above. Does he know he has a little bald spot on the back of his head?

'They will learn to live with your death just as they will learn to live with mine.' My father smiles at both of his friends. His eyes tell me he is saying goodbye without offering a single word. He loved them like brothers and I, uncles. There has never been a family occasion where these two were not in attendance. They may not be blood but they are still a part of the Prides no matter what.

'But who will avenge your murder?' I ask as my soul slowly begins to travel away from the car. Pumba pulls the van onto a driveway and speeds down towards a great big hangar at the end. The two of them scramble to get out with me in Pumba's arms and rush me inside.

"What took you two so long?!" a new voice booms, but from this distance I can't see who it is. Something that feels like ice is pressed against my back as Pumba lays me down. There is a sharp sting in the crook of my elbow and my spirit instinctively rubs the spot. Warmth begins to flood my veins from where I'm guessing they placed a needle.

'It's all part of the great big circle of life, my sweet girl. Uncle Scar will get what's coming to him. He has many enemies out there. Someone is

bound to turn on him like he did us.' My spirit slows at his words.

'What?! Uncle Scar didn't kill you! I saw Zira slit your throat with a knife! Uncle Scar didn't even move a muscle the entire time we were attacked!' I try to remember more details of their murder, but I get nothing. Maybe that's something only a person with a body can do.

"Her heartbeat is weak and she's lost a lot of blood. Call Viv at the blood bank and tell her I'll need four bags instead of two. Hopefully, she hasn't left yet," the new voice demands. A phone is unlocked next to my ear again before a dial tone sounds.

"Hey Viv, Raf needs four bags not two," Pumba says quickly. A woman angrily says something down the line before hanging up. "She just got in the car but she will run back and get it."

"Good, thankfully she's not too far away so it shouldn't take her long to get here," Raf says to the others as he starts digging around in my chest. Fuck that hurts!

'Uncle Scar may not have lifted a finger but he definitely orchestrated the attack. There is no one else who wanted to control the Prides more than

him.' Did he turn on us for power? His own flesh and blood. I stop mid-air and look down at the warehouse. I thought I could go and everything would be okay, but it won't. No one will face up to Scar, not when he has Zira by his side. I have to go back. I may not be as strong as she is now, but I can be. It is I who must avenge my parents' deaths. I will take back what is rightfully mine and I have a feeling I know just where to start.

Chapter 3

Breaking news from Channel Eight in Silver Rock. Good evening, I am Zazu Hornbill reporting to you live from Ancient Tree Arena. Tonight, hundreds witnessed the murder of not one but three high ranking Pride family members. Mufasa, known more prominently as the ringleader for the Pride family fortune, was shot dead while he sat in his seat. His daughter-in-law Nala as well as his son Simba were also brutally murdered. We have confirmation that their daughter Kiara Pride was also with them tonight, however she has yet to be found. A witness told Channel Eight that she was last seen being carried out of the arena by a tall young man with jet-black hair, however this has yet to be confirmed.

Police have yet to give a statement as to who they are looking for however we will keep you updated with proceedings from this moment forward. I am Zazu Hornbill for Channel Eight news.

Chapter 4

Kiara age 22

My legs burn with a fire I've grown to love. It fuels my inner rage for those who stole my family from me. It has been six years since that dreadful night and I have not stopped pushing my body to its limits getting myself ready for the day I take everything back. Timon and Pumba told me to let it go. That I should be grateful that I barely escaped with my life. Like that would stop me. My bullet wound stings as the memory of my father falling to the ground comes forth and I push my legs to move even faster. I will not allow this hill to break me, or anything else for that matter.

My uncle killed everyone I ever loved just to gain control over one of the largest mafia groups in the world. He will get what's coming to him, they all will.

I run the last few steps and feel a sense of accomplishment the moment I reach the top. Finally! I raise my fists to the sky and throw my head back. I'm ready Dad, I'm ready to take back what is ours.

I steady my breathing as I turn around and begin to make my way back down the mountain towards the compound. Raf will be shitty that I'm late for training but hopefully his mood will change when I tell him that I conquered the mountain.

Pumba's van pulls up beside the compound the moment I enter the parking lot.

"What's up old man?" I ask punching his arm when he gets closer, he rubs the spot pretending that it hurt. Pumba is a wall of muscle—to be honest, I doubt much would affect him, especially a punch from little ole me.

"Not much, kiddo. Raf said you're still on track for Saturday." Pumba quickens his step, moving slightly in front of me, and opens the door. I smile at him as I step over the threshold.

"Damn straight I am. I'm ready to rock this shit." Pumba follows me in and we stop dead in our tracks the second we notice all the lights are off. Huh? Raf never turns them off no matter what time of day it is. I draw my gun from its holster at my side and hold it up.

"You go find the power box, I'll wait right here," I say, never taking my eyes off the wide open space in front of me.

"Ah, I don't..." he starts but I cut him off.

"Go Pumba, Raf could be hurt and we can't see shit!" Without another word, he bolts out the door. Finally!

My eyes slowly adjust to the darkness and I begin to make my way further into the hangar. My feet shuffle quietly along the floor as I tune my ears to listen for even the faintest sound. I breathe shallow breaths, never making a noise. I hear Pumba outside grunting as he tries to pry the electricity box open. That man can wield a sword like no one else I've ever seen but when it comes to ordinary tasks like this, he is hopeless.

I move my body around a huge pillar in the middle of the room as I make my way towards the centre of our arena. I stop when I hear the faintest sound of footsteps approaching from my right. I breathe in hard and raise my weapon. The smell of leather and wood hits my nose and I release my finger off the trigger just as the lights flick back on.

"Boom," Kovu says proudly, standing next to me. His fingers are in the shape of a gun which are pressed against my forehead. The barrel of my weapon is also aimed directly against his.

"You're fucking stupid, you know that? If it wasn't for your disgusting cologne I would have blown your head off." I narrow my eyes and stare at the man who saved my life. Raf told me I should trust him but something within me tells me not to. His mother was the one who murdered my family, after all.

"Yeah but you didn't though, so..." He shrugs, lowering his pretend weapon and walks off, heading towards our kitchen.

"What the fuck are you even doing here, Kovu? Where's Raf?" I stomp after him. I hate the fact that he let himself in here once again—he's done it three times this month. It was almost a year after the death of my parents that I saw Kovu again. He showed up here one day unannounced and Raf had to hold me back. I wanted to hurt him the same way his mother hurt me. I wanted to cause him unfathomable pain, like no matter how much time passed he still couldn't move past it or forget it. Half of me is thankful that he saved my life that day, but the other half wants him dead just because of who his mother is. He is just lucky Raf was here to save him.

"He's at the clinic with Viv, I just left him. He said he would be back soon and that I should meet him here." Kovu enters the kitchen, swipes an apple from the table and plonks his ass down on the first chair he finds.

"Making yourself at home, are we?"

"You know it, kitty cat." He purrs as he winks. The nickname he gave me makes my skin crawl although I somewhat like the meaning behind it. He said I'm quiet when I move around, like a lioness on the hunt.

"Why did he say you should meet him here?" I ask, crossing my arms over my chest and leaning back against the wall. I'm not letting this asshole out of my sight.

"That's because he is your sparring partner for today," Raf states proudly as he walks through the door.

"What?!" we both ask, surprised. My gaze shoots over to Kovu, who's staring at Raf.

"You heard me. Kovu could do with some training before the weekend and Kiara, let's face it, you will be up against his mother. What better way to learn about your opponent than to fight her protégé?" Raf's right; unbeknown to Kovu's mother that he switched sides years ago, she's still been training him to fight. I bet he knows all her best moves. Let's see if the mole can teach me something before I stick a knife in his mother's throat.

Years ago, I asked him why he went against his family and switched sides. He got right in my face that day and said that he would never be able to trust them after what they did. He said that he knew something was going to happen, but he didn't know what. He got his mother to promise that I wouldn't get hurt, that I would be safe, but she went back on her word. He made a promise with the devil for me!

Zira would be still hunting me to this day if it weren't for a lookalike junkie whose body washed up in the river about a week after the attack. It was so waterlogged that there was no way to tell the difference between us.

"Come on man, I train every morning. You know this," Kovu grumbles before taking a bite out of his apple as he raises his dark eyes at me. I meet his stare and lift my chin ever so slightly.

"Well, this should be easy for you then," I say, smirking as I push away from the wall and head back out into the arena. I hate being so close to him but if this means I get to beat him up, I'm all in!

"Oh, this should be interesting," Timon declares, taking a seat on the outer rim. He's made sure he's got a perfect view of the mat. I place my gun on the table just outside the door and remove my knife from its sheath at my side. Bending down, I unlace my boots, sliding them off before arranging them neatly beside the mat. I may look like I have my shit together but my insides are reeling. It's been almost a year since we stepped onto the mat together. Who knows what his mother has taught him since then?

But if Raf has confidence in me, then so shall I. *Breathe Kiara, trust yourself,* my father's words echo through my mind.

"But Raf, what if I hurt her?" Kovu asks, trying to talk his way out of fighting me.

"My boy, I'm not afraid you will hurt her, more like she will hurt you. Kiara is ready, now I need to see if you are. Just don't kill each other, alright? You both need to be fit and ready to go on Saturday, got that Kiara?" Raf asks, giving me a stern look.

"Yes sir, although I will thoroughly enjoy kicking his ass." I smile at Kovu over my shoulder and walk onto the mat. Pumba takes a seat beside Timon and smiles as he digs into his bowl of popcorn. Of course, he's got snacks. I position myself in the middle of the ring and wait for his highness to join me. Damn, he is precious, is he afraid or something because he is taking forever to remove his shit.

"Hurry up already! Some of us have better things to do than wait around for your spoiled ass," I shout, crossing my arms over my chest. He glances over at me with fire in his eyes. Just you wait, Kovu, I'll put that heat out quicker than you can say burn.

"I wouldn't be so cocky if I were you," he says, and my heartbeat picks up as he finally makes his way over. Kovu stops less than a metre away and rakes his eyes up and down my body. He pauses over my hips and my breasts before coming to a complete stop at my throat.

"What are you looking at?" I grumble and his eyes go wide when he realises he's been caught staring.

"Huh? Nothing," he says, shaking his head, and turns to look at Raf. Was he checking me out? I glance down at my attire and see nothing out of the ordinary. I'm wearing my tight black pants with a gun holster at my side and a corset with a white shirt underneath. To some it may look uncomfortable but to me, it's perfect.

"Okay you two, you know the rules. No eye gouging, no choking, no aiming for the privates. Just keep it clean or you'll be running laps until sundown. Got it?" Raf gives each of us a stern look and I know not to push it. A few years ago I ran around the compound for hours because I disrespected his rules. I won't be making that mistake twice. We both nod and ready ourselves to fight. I lift my arms and position them in front of me while Kovu moves one leg behind him and crouches low. Well, that's new.

"You ready?" Raf asks, looking over at me.

"Yep," I mutter, never taking my eyes off my opponent.

"You?" he asks Kovu, who just nods.

"Fight!" Raf drops his arm between us and steps back off the mat. I slowly shuffle forward knowing that any moment Kovu will probably swing his leg out and try to knock me off my feet. Bitch, I'm ready for you. I'm two feet away when he half cartwheels to the side, rests one hand on the floor and kicks me with both feet in the stomach. Oomph! For a second I am completely winded. I stumble backwards as he gets to his feet and charges forward. The moment he is within reach, I swing my fist up, punching him in the chin, making his head snap back. Kovu takes a few quick steps backwards, holding the side of his face as a round of cheers sounds from the sidelines.

"Woohoo, go Kiara!" Timon calls. A smile plays in the corner of my lips as I watch Kovu's eyes darken.

"You're going to pay for that," he seethes, wiping blood from the side of his mouth.

"Give it your best shot." I ready myself, moving my legs apart, preparing for whatever he will throw my way. Kovu charges forward with his hands balled into fists. I raise my arms, protecting my face, however Kovu goes low. I pull an arm back ready to hit him again but this time he's faster. He barrels right into me, knocking us both to the ground. I lay a few punches to his stomach and his ribs, loving the pain that ignites in my knuckles from every confirmed hit. I manage to get the upper hand and straddle him as I lay blow for blow on the sides of his face. My heart is racing as I know I am about to win this match. Sweat runs down the sides of my face and drips onto the ground beside me.

"Enough!" Kovu growls as he moves one leg up, hooks it around my upper body and rips me off his lap. I barely have time to react when Kovu scrambles on top of me. He grabs both my wrists, secures them tightly above my head and peers down into my eyes. His face is so close I can feel his breath on my skin. My heart begins pounding for a whole new reason.

"I know I'm pretty babe but you need to stop aiming for my face." He smiles a full smile although the sides of his face are already breaking out into big red welts. "It's already going to be hard enough to explain to my mother how I got the bruises on my ribs." He must be in pain but his face doesn't show it.

"How are you going to explain it?" I ask almost breathlessly. I swallow past the lump forming in my throat and scream at myself for acting this way. He's just a guy, Kiara, a very hot guy who... who... whose family murdered mine. Yeah, that's it... remember that? But he saved my life when he wasn't supposed to. I stare up into his big brown eyes and wonder why he went against his mother's wishes and got me out all those years ago.

"I'll think of something," he mutters, never taking his eyes off mine. He takes a deep breath in and slightly presses his body closer against mine. I feel something hard pressing against my inner thigh and have to switch my thoughts to anything other than his cock touching me.

"I bet you will," I retort, glancing stupidly down at his lips. They are so perfect and plump, so utterly kissable. No, Kiara! Stop this. Your first kiss will not be with the man who... who. My train of thought leaves the station when Kovu leans down and presses his lips to mine. Oh my god! My heart skips a beat not knowing whether to flee or fight. His kiss is soft and warm. He slides one of my arms closer to the other and fixes himself so he's holding both of my wrists together with one hand. He lowers the other to my throat and raises my chin with his thumb. I open my mouth allowing him access and he begins to massage my tongue with his. He tastes like a sweet apple but also somehow salty. A small moan vibrates in my throat and Kovu smiles against my lips.

"You like that, kitty cat?" he asks and I nod before he places his lips back down upon mine. The notion is so arousing, my core feels all warm and gooey. I shift my legs out from beneath him and wrap them around his waist.

Kovu groans inwardly. He removes his hand from around my throat and begins to slide it down my body. His whole body freezes when he reaches my breast and I feel his terror radiating off him. It's like being struck by lightning the speed he rips his head away from mine and begins to check our surroundings. FUCK! The guys!

I wiggle my body enough that Kovu releases my arms and I flip him onto his back. The thought of what I just did in front of them is like a bucket of cold water over my body. How could I let myself get so distracted?

I jump to my feet and look at Timon and Pumba, but they are gone and so is Raf. My heart hammers in my chest as my eyes dart around the room. I didn't even hear them leave.

"They're gone, Kiara," he says, less than three feet behind me.

"No shit Sherlock," I mutter, not having the courage to look at him. How are we going to get through Saturday now? For fuck's sake Kiara, how could you let yourself be so stupid?

"Kiara..." he starts but I cut him off.

"Just stop, Kovu," I say over my shoulder. "We shouldn't have done that. What we just did was a mistake. We have to remain focused on the task and that's all." I need to leave and that's what I'll do. I head for the hangar door and don't look back. Maybe it wasn't hatred I was feeling for him all these years but something else entirely. Who knows—but whatever it is, I don't like it.

Chapter 5

"Are you ready?" Raf asks as he enters the armoury. I have all my weapons laid out on the table in front of me. I need to check each one to make sure it's loaded before I storm Pride tower later this afternoon. I grab a magazine off the table and insert it into my gun before placing my weapon back on the table.

"I was born ready, Raf." I grab a knife next and remove it from its sheath. I flick my thumb over the edge of the blade, checking its sharpness. Timon told me earlier that Pumba was down here last night checking all my weapons too. He's worried about the outcome of today's antics, so to give himself some peace of mind, he made sure everything was in order before I even had a look myself.

"I know you were, Kiara. You wouldn't be a Pride if you weren't. Just remember to never turn your back on them, not even for a second. Always shoot first and ask questions later. To..." Okay, that's enough.

"I know, Raf. Don't fret, I've got this and I'll be back here before you know it."

"But I do worry, Kiara, you are going up against not only your great uncle Scar but also Zira. Silver Rock's number one assassin. She is the best of the best..." He trails off as he stares at the blank wall behind me. Raf is beginning to doubt my competence for this mission. That's not good considering I leave in a matter of hours.

"Well, all I can say, Raf, is that I'll give it my best shot. If I die while trying to retrieve what is rightfully mine, then so be it." I pick up my duffle bag from the floor and throw my weapons in. Why couldn't he just come in here and tell me I'm going to be great, why did he have to say that shit making me doubt myself? I grit my teeth as I force myself to say no more. My god, he pissed me off.

"Kiara..."

"Just leave me alone Raf, I have to finish preparing myself to die." I glance up at him only for a moment before returning to the task at hand. He obviously sees the anger in my eyes and does as he's told, walking back out the same way from which he came.

I throw my last gun into the bag and let out a frustrated sigh. Don't listen to him Kiara, he is just scared. Zira is a nasty piece of work but if I can take down all the guys here with ease, then I can take her down too. I just hope nothing else is standing in my way when push comes to shove.

"Kovu said he will meet you at the back entrance. It will be the easiest way to sneak you in undetected," Timon says over his shoulder as we near Pride Tower. I stare at what was once my home through the windscreen. With its blacked-out windows and its one hundred and eighty stories, it seriously is the tallest tower in all of Silver Rock.

I wanted to go in guns blazing and show these men who they were messing with, but all the guys contested that, especially Kovu. They said it would be safer for me if no one knew I was coming and I went straight to the top to only take out those who were necessary, but in my eyes, they are all targets. They all stood behind my uncle and allowed Zira access to the Pride family fortune. Like she'll ever be a part of the family.

The memory of Kovu's lips on my skin enters my mind and my body instantly feels warm. I haven't seen him since that day and honestly, I don't know how I feel about that. We have always had it out for each other, but maybe it was something else entirely.

"Whatever you're thinking about girly, let it go. You need your head in the game." Raf glares at me from across the van. After our minor disagreement this morning we haven't spoken much today. I don't want to hear any more doubt spewing from his lips.

"My head never left the game, Raf, I've been ready for this for over a year now. You're the one who keeps pushing the date back." I remove my gun from the holster at my side and double-check the mag. Still fully loaded, just how I left it. I load the mag back into the gun and stow it away at my side.

For something as scary as what I'm about to do, I am unreasonably calm. The men around me, however, are visibly shaking in their boots. They wanted to join me on this mission but I told them no, I need to do this alone. The only reason I am allowing Kovu to tag along is because he is my way in. Otherwise, he would have been told to fuck off too. I just hope he remembers who he's fighting for, especially when it comes down to me and his mother.

Pumba sharply turns the corner and I have to quickly brace myself against the side of the van to stop myself from falling over.

"Whoever approved your licence, Pumba, needs to have theirs revoked. Your driving sucks," I grumble as I release the tension in my leg. I'm not joking either. It amazes me that he's never had an accident.

"I love you too kiddo." A small smile plays on my lips at his words. It's not very often that someone says they love me. I know they all do in their own way. We are a family, after all. I just wish the other half of mine was around to see what I'm about to do. My father's blood-stained face enters my mind but I quickly shake it away. That is not something I want to see right about now.

Raf slides his phone out of his pocket and dials a number. "Are you in position?" he asks as the receiver answers the call. I try to hear what Kovu has to say but it's muffled over the sound of Pumba's diesel engine. "Good, we are coming up to the door now," Raf says, hanging up the phone as Pumba rounds another sharp corner. This time I'm not as prepared and fall forward, smacking my head on the metal door in front of me. I scream out in pain as I quickly correct myself and check to see if there is any blood. For fuck's sake man! Is he trying to kill me so they won't, my god! Thankfully I'm okay but I swear I will have a killer bump on my forehead in a second.

"You good Kiara?" Pumba asks over his shoulder, never taking his eyes off the laneway.

"I will be when I can get out of the van." Only two more blocks to go, then I'm free of this hell trap.

"Ha, you're funny." He snickers.

"So is your driving. Geez Pumba fucking slow down or you're going to drive straight past the building," I yell.

"Oh shit sorry." Pumba slams on the brakes, stopping directly behind Pride Tower. A great oomph leaves my mouth when my back slams against the metal wall behind me. Thank god that's over. Timon and Pumba turn around to watch me leave. I feel their sorrows, I know they don't want me to go and yet they know why I must. This is my life's mission. I am to either storm the gates and take back what's mine or at least die trying.

Raf reaches out his hand and gives me his favourite pocketknife. He never goes anywhere without this thing. It was the last gift my father gave him before he died.

"Raf I can't," I mutter, not wanting it. Raf, on the other hand, doesn't give me the choice as he reaches out with his other hand and forcefully places the hilt of the blade in my palm. Although I know I must go, my heart breaks thinking I may never see these three again.

"You must Kiara, your father would want you to have it." My eyes well with unshed tears as I stare down at the lion carved into the wood.

"I know he's looking out for me from above but my god I miss him." A single tear slides down the side of my face and I internally slap myself for being so vulnerable. Get your shit together Kiara, you're about to storm Pride Tower for crying out loud.

"He is with you every step of the way, now get going kid. We don't want to attract any unwanted attention."

"Like the big blue van isn't doing that already," I retort under my breath as I stare at the two men up front.

"Knock 'em dead kiddo," Timon says with a brave smile. I know he is smiling more for himself than for me. He is such a softy sometimes.

"Use your head, don't think before you act and never let your emotions get in the way," Pumba proclaims and I nod. I get up from my position on the floor and slide open the door.

"You know I truly love you guys. Thank you for putting up with my sorry ass for all these years." I swing my bag over my shoulder as the door to Pride Tower opens behind me. Kovu sticks his head out, waving me over and I don't wait for a reply as I sprint over to him.

"I thought you were super close, so what the fuck took you so long?" Kovu quietly grumbles behind me as he fastens the door shut. It's pitch black and I can't see shit. I feel him next to me and my inside begin to quiver. Deep breaths Kiara, you can do this. He smells of something that only rich people would wear, it's strong and yet also sweet.

"Well, if you must know, I was saying goodbye." Well, not really goodbye, but he doesn't have to know that.

"Women," he mutters as he grabs my hand and begins pulling me god knows where. I'm about to protest when I remember where I am. I lighten my footsteps against the stone flooring, hoping to god that Kovu doesn't run me into a wall.

"Stairs," he whispers somewhere in front of me as he slows down our pace. I feel his arm rise higher and know he is moving up. I move my foot around, feeling for a step. Where are you? I know you're here somewhere. I hit something hard with my foot and my whole body fills with anticipation. Got it! We begin to climb the stairs as quickly as we can, reaching the second landing in record time. There is poor lighting up here too but thankfully Kovu knows his way around.

We race to the end of a long hallway and turn the corner. Kovu slows down and stops in front of these huge wooden doors. I glance up at their beauty as he fiddles with some keys and for a second I'm hit with a wave of nostalgia. I know this room. My father's dazzling smile comes into view as he reads me a book in front of a fireplace. It was winter and the power was out but thankfully my father had a few fireplaces installed when he modified Pride Tower before I was born.

"This was my parents' room," I mutter under my breath as Kovu places the key into the hole and unlocks the doors. They open inward and he rushes us inside. Once we are past the threshold he quickly turns around and locks them again.

"The guards are in the middle of changing their rounds upstairs. We have maybe two hours before the new ones set in. We can use the tunnels from here or..." I zoned out the moment we entered the room. So many memories came flooding in that I couldn't hold back the tears that were bound to fall. My mother's golden hair blew in the afternoon breeze that came through the open window. I jumped on their bed although I knew I wasn't allowed to. Kovu and I played hide and seek with my parents when his mother disappeared on a mission. That happened almost every day.

"Kiara," Kovu calls bringing me back to the here and now. I shake my memories away, not needing them to distract me any more than they already have. "I know this is hard for you but get your head in the game!" he growls as he crosses his arms. He's right, now is not the time to get lost in my own thoughts.

"Sorry. You were saying." Kovu just stares at me and I see the moment he lets his anger go. His eyes slowly soften as he lets out a sigh. He never could stay angry with me for long, it's always been one of his downfalls.

"I was saying the rotation upstairs is almost up and the new guards will be coming soon. I recommend that we wait here for half an hour or so to allow the old guards the time to exit the building. There will be fewer people up there if we wait." I contemplate my options but know he is probably right. Although this was once my home, a lot has changed since then.

"Okay, let's do that, but I'm not waiting here…" Especially not alone with him in his room. "I want to be up there when it's time to go."

"Deal, I just hope those boots of yours don't hurt your feet because we have one hell of a climb on our hands." He smirks down at my knee-high lace-up boots as if these things will stop me. Bitch I train in these. I would bet all the money I have that these are way more comfortable than anything he wears.

"Bring it on." I accept the challenge and follow him over to the secret passageway hidden in the left wall.

Chapter 6

We finally reach the seventieth floor and I'm exhausted. Fuck this shit! I will not climb another step. I know there is a service elevator at the end of the hallway and I don't care anymore if someone catches us. I'm ready for them.

Sweat lines my brows and my breaths are laboured. I glance over at Kovu and see he is tired too. Whoever thought that climbing the entire building was a good idea is just stupid. This thing is one hundred and eighty stories high! We got to seventy and my body feels like it's about to collapse. My thighs and ass burn with every step I take. How the hell am I going to take out the leader of the Pride when all I want to do is sleep?

'Remember who you are, Kiara,' my father's voice filters through my mind. He sounded so close this time and although I know he isn't there, I can't help glancing over my shoulder. My quick movements catch Kovu's attention.

"What is it? Did you hear something?" he asks quietly. He too glances over his shoulder as we quickly make our way to the end of the hall and into the elevator. I rest my back against the cool metal as Kovu presses the button for the top floor. The doors close in front of us and for a second I allow myself to relax.

'Be who you were born to be, my dear sweet Kiara,' this time it's my mother's voice which sends chills running down my spine. I haven't heard her voice at all since the day she passed away. It sounds so different to what I remember.

"What happened just now? You have a sad look on your face," Kovu asks, resting his back against the elevator opposite me. I glance up at the numbers on the wall which are climbing the higher we move and contemplate telling him about the voices. I wonder if he will believe me or just think I'm crazy. I'm hoping it's the first one.

"Now and again I hear my father's voice in my head. I don't know if he's speaking to me from the other side or if it's something I remember from long ago. His voice always tends to come when I need him the most, but this time I heard my mother's. It was the first time I heard her voice since the day she died." Kovu's eyes turn down with sadness remembering the day he saved my life. He risked his own neck to get me out of there and then lied to his mum about it. He told her he put me down outside the venue and then I vanished. Like, as if she would believe that.

Zira is Silver Rock's best hunter, I have no doubt she checked all the cameras and knew he was lying. Perhaps she just wanted to keep it a secret because if Scar ever found out what Kovu had done, he would have been dead too. He's just lucky the junkie washed up around the same time and she stopped looking for me.

"I bet they are trying to guide you on the right path. Scar talks about his all the time, your ancestors

I mean. He says they help him make the right decision. Whether that is true or not, I have no idea, but if you're hearing your parents, then maybe it is." He looks up at me and our eyes connect. So much passes between us in that short moment that I don't even know what to say anymore. If only I weren't a Pride and he wasn't Zira's son, maybe then there could have been something more between us. His lips pressed against mine filters through my thoughts and my lips tingle, wanting to feel it again. "Kiara," he says, and my eyes snap up to his. "Whatever happens later, whatever you hear, just remember I am with you every step of the way." What does that mean? The elevator begins to slow and I push away from the wall, withdrawing my gun from its holster.

My heart hammers in my chest as the lift comes to a stop and the doors open slowly. I was praying to see maybe one or two guards on the other side but strangely it's empty. Huh? I glance over at Kovu, who shrugs, and we both exit the lift, doing a sweep of the corridors on either side. Nothing.

"Where is everyone? I thought you said the shift changed ages ago, so why are the hallways empty?" I ask quietly. We head down the hall towards my uncle's office, checking every room we pass. Maybe he's not here, maybe he left and that's why there are no guards around.

"It did. What the fuck is going on?" He glances behind us but no one is there. He turns back, shaking his head, and curses under his breath. I can tell he's frustrated as so am I. I have trained for this day for years. For fucking years! What the fuck am I supposed to do now if there is no one here to fight? Just sit inside his office and wait for him to return?

We get to the grand double doors on the other end of the hall and I press my back against the door. Kovu counts to three and opens her up.

"What have I told you about playing with guns Kovu, knives are so much better." My heart stops at the sound of my uncle's voice. He's here. He's actually here!! What the fuck!

"About damn time you showed up! Did you seriously think we would wait here all night for you?" Zira's voice sounds impatient. Did he set this up? My eyes shoot daggers into the side of his face but Kovu doesn't take his eyes off those inside the room.

"Sorry Uncle Scar. I know you prefer knives but I kind of like this thing," Kovu says, raising his gun and tilting it from side to side. He toys with it like he's never held a real gun before.

"Why did you have your weapon drawn anyway boy? You knew we would be in here." He what? My eyes widen as my blood boils. Did he just lead me into a fucking trap? Is that what this is? As quickly as I can I begin to weigh up my options. Do I burst in there hoping my aim is as good as I think it is and try and shoot them dead, or do I wait a bit and see where this goes? Fuck, I don't know.

"Actually, I forgot about this, ah… meeting." He stumbles over his words while standing in the doorway. Why is he acting so weird? If Zira catches on that something is off she will come over and all of my years of training will be thrown out the window. "But that doesn't matter," he continues. "Where are the guards? I've never seen this floor so dead," he asks, finally stepping inside the office. I tune my ears to hear more than just the three people inside the room. I listen out for any other footsteps or even the sound of someone breathing. Thankfully there is nothing.

"We sent them home, Scar didn't want them to overhear our conversation," Zira says as a matter of fact.

"Come sit down boy." My uncle's voice filters out through the open door. I have to stop myself from barging into the office and putting a bullet in his brain. Kovu walks across the room and takes a seat.

"So what's this all about?" Kovu asks with a hint of defiance in his voice. I risk a peek around the edge of the door and see my uncle, the sick bastard and his show pony of an assassin sitting at a desk on the far side of the room. Kovu has his leg braced upon his knee as he sits confidently across from the man who orchestrated the attack on my parents. I pull back and press myself against the door. How can I get inside without them noticing? If only I could sneak up behind my uncle, then I could kill him with the weapon he loves the most. A knife to the throat is the perfect outing for a man as vile as him.

They'll never see you coming,' my father says. What does he mean by that? An image follows my father's words, a painting of a lion attacking another male pops into view. I remember that picture, but where do I know it from?

"As you know, Kovu, Scar has been unwell lately and he has something he wants to tell you," Zira says on the other side of the door, drawing my attention back to the here and now. There is a long pause before the sound of leather creaking echoes around the quiet room.

"My boy, I am dying. The doctors believe I have stage four cancer or some shit, but I don't care. I am old and I am done. That is why I am signing the Pride fortune over to you. Zira has trained you well and I believe you'll be the next ruthless leader this foundation deserves," Scar croaks out like he has no breath left inside his pathetic body. Heat races through my veins at his words. He is going to leave what is rightfully mine to KOVU! My breaths come quickly as I try to control my rage. Cool it, Kiara, you don't want to expose yourself now. I just need a way in! I risk another glance into the room beyond the door and I can't believe what I see. Right there on the far wall, some distance away from the rest of them is the fucking painting!

Oh my gosh, how could I have forgotten! I push away from the door and as quietly as I can, I make my way into the next room. My father built a secret passageway out of the office in case of an emergency. Grandfather thought it was stupid but now it will be my way in. I close the door behind me but not all the way as I don't want the click to alert the huntress in the next room.

I run over to the far wall and press my ear up against it. Although their voices are muffled I can still make out every word.

"I understand that mother..." Kovu says, and I must have missed something in the two seconds I was gone. "...but my only question is why are you not taking over the Pride fortune yourself?" There is anger in his husky voice. My insides quiver just hearing the roughness of it. Get it together Kiara. You need to find the door. I run my palm along the smooth surface looking for the small round button. Where is it?

"Because I am better off fighting those who want to kill you my boy..." I halt my movements. Although Kovu is about to receive what is rightfully mine, would I have the heart to kill him for it? "...I am a hunter Kovu, I'm not someone who sits behind a desk," Zira says as a matter of fact. Like her son is anything other than just like her. Although Kovu wouldn't be able to sit and watch his disciples getting hurt. He may be Zira's son, but he has one thing she doesn't: a heart.

"I don't need you to fight for me, mother. I can do that myself. I was trained by the best, after all."

"Yes, and I have no doubt you will do well my boy, we just can't take any risks."

"So that is that, the throne is yours. Sign here," Scar announces as my fingers brush against the button. Finally, I push it in and thankfully the door opens outwards with barely any sound. I climb through the small doorway and shut the door behind me. It's two small steps to the other side and I find the handle for the latch immediately. My fingers grasp the cool metal and for a moment I stop. My pulse hammers in my ears for what I'm about to do but I would rather die trying than do nothing at all. They don't deserve to live for what they put me and my family through. A life for a life.

The painting hangs directly behind Zira and Scar so hopefully I'll be able to slip into the room undetected. There is a fifty-fifty chance Zira will hear me and kill me before I even step out of the hideout, but fingers crossed that doesn't happen.

I withdraw my blade from my side, taking a deep breath in as I pull the lever. The wall falls inwards and I slightly push the painting outwards, making my way into the room. I slide my legs out first, feeling my way around the carpeted floor. I move the painting a little more and manoeuvre my body through the thin gap. My skin scrapes against the old wood, it's dry and splintered. Thankfully my clothes don't snag.

I move around the painting until I am free and as soon as I see them, my heart stops. Scar's grey hair shines like an aluminium plate under the weight of the white lights above him. Although most of Zira's skin is covered some of her murderous tattoo can still be seen poking out from beneath her halter neck.

Kovu and I lock eyes for a millisecond and I know he is warning me about what might go down. He is fully aware of what his mother is capable of. She didn't get the reputation of being the baddest cat in town for nothing.

I lower my breathing and take a step forward. Zira's first. I'm going to kill her the same way she killed my father, a knife to the throat.

Kovu grabs the pen off the table and signs his name on the dotted line.

"So what now?" he asks, leaning back in his chair, and rests his ankle on his knee. Kovu doesn't pay me another glance as he stares at his mother and Scar on the opposite side of the table.

My steps are light as I slowly make my way over to the person I have only dreamed about killing for years. I'm so close I can smell her scent, rosewood and cigarettes.

"For now, my son, you just sit back and relax while I take care of the little issue closing in on my back." My heart stops as Kovu's eyes dart to mine as his mother jumps to her feet. I swing my blade towards her but she ducks and knocks me off my feet.

"Kiara!" Kovu screams as his mother rushes over, grabs my hair, yanks me to my feet and places my knife at my throat. FUCK!

Scar spits at the ground beside him. "I fucking knew she wasn't dead. I could feel it in my bones. How could you lie to me boy?" His fury makes my insides shrink back. I bet if he were younger he would have Kovu on the ground in seconds.

"I..." Kovu starts not knowing what to say. His eyes are glued on the blade pressed up against my skin. With one quick swipe from Zira I would begin to bleed out and fall to the floor to die.

"You are not worthy of the Pride name," Zira seethes through gritted teeth and I feel the blade nick my skin. Kovu's eyes darken as droplets of my blood slide down my neck. All I need is a distraction, then I might be able to make my move.

"I don't need the name to do this." Kovu withdraws his gun from its holster and pulls the trigger. For a second my heart stops when I notice Kovu was aimed at me. Zira screams in my ear and slightly falls to her side clenching her knee. She drops the blade in her hand as another boom ricochets throughout the room. I don't have time to look up as I whirl around and snatch the knife out of Zira's hand, plunging the blade deep within her sternum. She makes a choking, gurgling sound as her eyes roll back in her head. Her limp body falls to the floor and I can't help but stare as her blood leaks from her body. All these years I have dreamt about this moment and it's finally here. I can't believe I did it. I kind of wanted something a little longer than that but I fucking killed her!

The sound of a person gurgling behind me has my muscles contracting. Oh god please no. With my weapons hot, I quickly turn back around, afraid of what I am about to face. Kovu has his eyes locked on the floor behind me as he is not the one making the horrible sounds. Scar sits on the opposite side of the table with a two-centimetre hole in his neck. His head has fallen back and rests against his chair behind him. Blood spews from the open wound and I have no doubt it won't take him long until he's dead too.

I glance back to where Kovu is staring and wonder if I should say anything. If it wasn't for him I might not be here right now.

"I know now is not the best time but thanks. I wouldn't have gotten out of that without your help." I cross my arms over my chest, not really sure what else to do right now. Kovu steers his attention away from his dead mother and lets out a huff of defeat.

"I wouldn't let her kill you. She may have been my mother but god I hated her. The moment she drew blood I knew what I had to do. Once you were free, I had to take away the other person in the room who wanted you dead. So I shot him too." Kovu locks eyes with the bullet wound in Scar's neck and smirks knowing he killed one of the most fearsome leaders in all of Silver Rock.

"If you hated your mother, why didn't you just kill her yourself?" I glance down at her knee and notice her kneecap is completely obliterated. No wonder she dropped to the ground so quick. I would have too.

"And what, take away a dream of yours? I don't think so. Zira was your mission, not mine, however you never mentioned how you would kill Scar, so I did it for you," he says proudly.

"Fair enough, so what do we do now?" I feel freer than I have in a very long time. The possibilities are endless.

"That decision is all yours, I just hope you keep me around to see it." Kovu declares with a sly smile. My insides flutter with anticipation for what our future holds. I would be stupid not having someone like him by my side. As I gaze into Kovu's eyes, I realise we may have had our differences in the past but after today and what he did for me, that is not something I'll ever be able to forget.

"We rebuild, we get rid of all the shit that tarnishes the Pride family name and make this foundation better than it's ever been before. Together, we will pave a new path, one that shines with integrity and honour. We will become a beacon of hope and inspiration for generations to come. With unity and perseverance, we will write a new chapter of greatness, one that will be remembered for all time." Kovu's eyes twinkle with understanding and warmth as he nods in response.

With Kovu by my side, I know that together we can navigate any challenges that come our way. The good and the bad. We just need to get rid of these dead bodies first.

The End

Ruthless Pride

Acknowledgements

Firstly, I would like to say a huge thank you to my Husband Robby. If it wasn't for you babe, I don't think I would ever have had the courage to get this far, so, thank you. x

Secondly, I would like to thank my mother, Cindy and my sister Loz for encouraging me to finish this story! I was a little unsure if I would get it done on time so thank you for the push.

Thank you to Ash Kim and Liv Evans for offering to help me out when I needed it so I could write. I really appreciated the offer.

Lastly thank you to you amazing readers! I hope you enjoyed Kiara and Kovu's story! I had a blast writing it.

Until next time

Always finding love within the darkness

Kristen

x

Follow Me

I would love to hear from you!

You would seriously make my day if you got in contact with me on my social media pages.

You can find me on Facebook – Author Kristen Dovnik. I'm on here quiet regularly.

I'm also on Instagram – authorkristendovnik

I'm frequently on here.

And for those of you who do not have social media you can find me at my website. www.kristendovnik.com

You can also join my reader group on Facebook to stay up to date on what's happening.

I hope to hear from you soon.

X

www.ingramcontent.com/pod-product-compliance
Lightning Source LLC
Chambersburg PA
CBHW030418120726
47904CB00007B/2325